The Loogie the Booger Genie

A VERY NASTY COLD

By N.E. Castle

Illustrated by
Bret Herholz and N.E. Castle

D1301487

For Edward, who shares my sense of humor.

Table of Contents

1.
Play Day

One Saturday morning a ray of sunlight slid across Charlie's eyes. It woke him from a pretty cool dream. He was learning to turn frogs into cats and cats into lizards. Loogie had been

teaching him. It was lots of fun, but it was just a dream. Only Loogie could do magic.

Charlie Simms was eight years old. He was just like every other third grader, except that his closest friend,

Loogie, was a genie—and a prince. Charlie had found Prince Loogar's bottle in the ruins of old Garoth Castle in England. A cranky old wizard had turned the prince into a genie and trapped him in his bottle 805 years earlier.

Unfortunately, Charlie had managed to get Loogar's bottle stuck in his nose (it was a very tiny bottle). Charlie had tried everything to pull the bottle out, but it was no use. Loogar's bottle was stuck by magic.

Saturdays were Charlie's favorite day. Unfortunately, on this Saturday, his throat was dry and scratchy. He drank some water, but it didn't help much. His nose tickled and his eyes watered. Charlie thought the tickle might be Loogar—he tickled Charlie's nose when he wanted to come out.

Charlie rubbed his nose. The genie whooshed out in a puff of smoke. He rolled his eyes and smirked.

"Today is Saturday, right?" Loogar asked snobbishly. "I suppose you will wish me to play some silly game." He flew over to the window. His tether, a thin wisp of smoke that prevented him from flying much more than a few feet from Charlie's nose, tightened and yanked Charlie off his bed. "Oh, do keep up, peasant," he sighed.

"Yes, it's play day. Keep quiet so Mom and Dad don't hear you. They think I'm always talking to myself," Charlie said with a sniffle.

"I am a prince. I will speak as I choose to speak," Loogar huffed.

"Fine, just do it quietly!" Charlie retorted.

"Charlie! Breakfast is ready," his mother called from downstairs.

"Shhh. Get back in my nose," Charlie said, and Loogar was instantly sucked back into his nostril. Charlie winced. It felt like a baseball had been stuffed into his nose. He sniffled and hurried downstairs.

Charlie drank his hot chocolate (he loved hot chocolate with Saturday breakfast). His mom had made him chocolate chip pancakes too.

Suddenly his nose itched. Charlie scratched it once and continued with his breakfast. Soon his nose itched again, so Charlie scratched twice. He was careful to only scratch once or twice. Whenever he scratched or rubbed his nose, he rubbed the genie bottle. Rubbing the genie bottle three times at once called Loogar out.

Charlie took a big bite of pancake and his nose tickled again. "Stop it!" he whispered.

Suddenly he sneezed once, then twice. He nearly spewed pancake across the table. Charlie swallowed his pancake quickly—just in time to sneeze again.

He finished his breakfast quickly and excused himself. He hurried to his bedroom and closed the door. Charlie rubbed his nose several times and Loogar appeared.

"Hey, I was enjoying my breakfast. Why did you tickle my nose?" Charlie asked the genie prince.

"I did no such thing," Loogar said. "Though I do think you were taking far too long to eat your breakfast. We do have games to play—even if they are peasant games that are hardly fit for a prince."

"But I haven't played with my friends on a Saturday in three weeks," Charlie said.

Loogar huffed. "But you have said that I am your friend. You should be honored to have a prince as your friend, peasant."

"You ARE my friend, Loogie, but I have other

friends too. I told Katie I would play with her this morning. She'll be over soon. You have to go back in your bottle."

Katie was one of Charlie's best friends. She was a tomboy in pink. She was as tough as any boy, but definitely a girl.

Loogar sulked, then darted into Charlie's nose. But when the genie was halfway into his

nostril, Charlie sneezed. He sneezed so hard that Loogar shot out of his nose and bounced off of the bed. The wisp of smoke connecting him to Charlie acted like a rubber band and snapped Loogar back into his nose. Charlie sneezed again and shot the genie across the room. When he bounced back, he hit Charlie squarely in the face and knocked him to the floor.

"What are you DOING, peasant?" Loogar screamed.

"Sneezing. I think I have a cold," Charlie sniffled.

"What is a cold?" Loogar asked. He clapped a hand over Charlie's mouth and nose before he could sneeze again.

"It's a virus that makes you cough and sneeze a lot. Haven't you ever had a cold?" Charlie asked.

Loogar turned up his nose. "Nonsense! A prince is above these peasantries. The wizard makes certain the royal family is always well."

"That's cool," Charlie replied. "But without magic, anybody can get a cold. Well, anybody except maybe a genie. Can you get sick?"

"Never!" Loogar scoffed.

"Lucky for you," Charlie said. "But when I'm sick, Mom lets me watch cartoons and makes me chicken soup."

"Chicken soup is for peasants," Loogar sneered.

"Well, then I'm glad to be a peasant, because I LOVE Mom's chicken soup."

Charlie sneezed again. This time he covered his mouth and nose so Loogar didn't get shot across the room.

"I'll take some cold medicine," Charlie sniffled. "It's downstairs. You'd better go back into my nose while I go get it."

"You'd better not sneeze again, and do keep QUIET. Your breathing is DREADFULLY loud!" Loogar warned. He darted cautiously up Charlie's nose and disappeared. Charlie sneezed three more times.

Charlie wanted to go out and play, but his mother wouldn't let him go outside if he wasn't feeling well. If he could stop sneezing, though, she wouldn't know he was sick.

He ran downstairs to the medicine cabinet. The cherry cold syrup was on the top shelf, just beyond his reach. He climbed noisily onto the counter.

His mother's voice came from right outside the bathroom door. "Charlie, are you all right?"

"Yes, Mom."

"I thought I heard you sneezing."

"Just a couple of times, but I'm OK," Charlie lied.

"Why don't you go outside and play?"

"OK." Charlie measured out the cherry syrup the way his mother had taught him and drank it.

2.

The Boy-Shaped Booger

It was chilly outside. Charlie shivered and zipped up his jacket.

Katie lived just down the street. She waved to him from her house, then rode over on her bike. She wore a bright pink jacket that was the same shade as her bike. Katie loved pink.

"You want to race around your house?" she asked.

"Sure," Charlie answered. They often raced their bikes. Charlie won most of the time, but today he wasn't as fast as usual. His cold made him tired. He pedaled fast, but Katie won the race by a whole ten feet.

"Want to go again?" Katie asked.

"Sure!" Charlie replied, and took off riding. Katie started late, several feet behind Charlie, but soon she caught up to him. She grinned at him, then pedaled past to win again.

"You're slow today," Katie said. "You should quit being nice. I can beat you on my own."

"I'm not being nice. I have a cold. I guess it has made me a little tired," Charlie said. His nose tickled and he sneezed at Katie.

"Ew!" Katie said as she backed up. "You sneezed on me."

"Sorry," Charlie said.

"Don't sneeze on me. I don't want to catch your cold."

"I'll try not to," Charlie said. "You want to play on the swings?" Charlie had two swings in his backyard. Actually, he had a whole play structure with a slide, a fort, and even a rock-climbing wall. The swings were his favorite part.

"Sure," Katie said.

Charlie's nose tickled and he scratched once. They climbed onto the swings. Soon they were racing to see who could swing the highest. Katie pushed Charlie sideways to slow him down. She swung higher and higher.

"Watch this!" Katie said. She jumped off when the swing was high in the air.

"I can beat that." Charlie pumped his swing higher and jumped off. He landed a foot beyond Katie's landing.

Charlie's nose suddenly tickled a LOT. The tickling made his eyes water. He rubbed his nose hard. Once, twice, three times he rubbed. Too late, he realized what he had done.

Loogar whooshed out of his nose. The genie nearly knocked Katie over.

"Do you want to play NOW, peasant?" Loogar demanded.

Charlie froze where he stood. He looked at Katie sheepishly.

"Charlie Simms! Who is that?" Katie shrieked.

"Ummm...it's Loogie," Charlie replied. His cheeks turned bright red and he shrugged. He shoved his hands in his pockets.

Katie was shocked a moment. Then she burst out laughing. "You have a boy in your nose?"

"Don't laugh," Charlie said.

"I can't help it. You have a boy-shaped booger!"

"I am NOT a booger," Loogar huffed. "I am a PRINCE."

"This is Loogie," Charlie said. "Loogie is a genie."

"PRINCE Loogar," he corrected. "Who is your maiden friend?" He gave Katie a princely smile.

"Katie," she answered. "Your name is Loogie?"

"My nanny, Miss Bellediddy, calls me Loogie," he said. "Your peasant friend does as well. But my name is Prince Loogar."

Katie laughed harder.

"What is funny?" Loogar asked.

"Sorry," she said. Katie bit her lip to stop laughing. She saw that Loogar didn't know—a loogie is a very large booger. If she were mean, she would have told him. But Katie wasn't a bully.

"How did you end up in Charlie's nose?" she asked.

Loogar told her how he had played a prank on Wizard Hendrick and how the wizard had turned him into a genie as punishment. He scowled as he explained that only good deeds could set him free. He had to right his wrongs. At least that was what Hendrick had told him.

The sky began to spit rain. The wind picked up.

"Let's go inside," Charlie said. "Loogie, you have to go back in your bottle."

Katie's eyes opened wide. She screeched as Loogar disappeared into Charlie's nose. It was a horrible thing to watch.

3.
Be Careful What You Wish

Inside the house they took off their coats and shoes. The air was warm after the chilly rain. Charlie sneezed several times.

"Charlie, do you have a cold?" his mother asked. "Would you like some hot chocolate and buttered toast? That should warm you both up." She disappeared into the kitchen.

Charlie and Katie sat down at the table. In a few minutes Mrs. Simms set two steaming mugs of cocoa in front of them, along with toast and jelly. "I'm going to the store," she said. "I'll be back in half an hour." They thanked her as she left.

Charlie dunked the buttered toast in his hot chocolate and nibbled the chocolaty ends. It was one of his favorite treats.

"You're weird, Charlie Simms," Katie said as she watched him. "You're supposed to eat toast with jelly." She spread a glob of jelly across her toast. "What happened to Loogie?"

"He's in my nose," Charlie replied.

"He lives there?" she asked. Charlie nodded. "Can he hear what we say?" He nodded again. "That's too weird."

Charlie's nose tickled, so he rubbed it. Loogar whooshed out with a scowl on his face.

"Do you have ANY idea how loud your sneezing is inside your nose?" the prince demanded. Charlie shook his head. "It is very loud. I do NOT wish to be stuck in your nose while you sneeze. Have you no idea what it is like to live in that bottle?"

Charlie shook his head.

"It's not a room for a prince, anyway. There is nowhere to sit, there is no light. It is a terrible space," Loogar complained.

"Oh," Charlie sniffled. And before he knew what he was doing, he said, "I wish I could see the inside of your bottle."

Genies can grant almost any wish, whether you really want what you wished for or not. Charlie's nose began to burn and hurt worse than ever! Even Loogar's comings and goings didn't hurt like this. He opened his mouth to scream. Then suddenly everything was dark.

Loogar stood beside him. Yes—Loogar was beside him! He was not a wisp of snot attached to Charlie's nose. He was standing on his own two feet.

"Wow! You're out of my nose," Charlie said. "You're out of your bottle!"

Loogar snorted with laughter. "No. I do

believe we are now BOTH in your nose. We are both in my bottle," he corrected.

"That's impossible," Charlie said. "I can't be inside my own nose."

"It seems that it IS possible," Loogar said. "My magic is quite powerful. You should be glad my bottle has no mirror."

"What do you mean? What do I look like?" Charlie put his hands to his face. What his hands touched was not his face at all. It was slimy, drippy, and gross. He was touching the inside of his own nose.

Charlie screamed. "Yikes! I wish I was back to normal!"

Instantly he was standing next to Katie. She looked pale. She would have looked better if she had seen a ghost.

Charlie's nose really hurt! He rubbed it gently. Loogar eased out slowly, wearing a very malicious grin.

"That must have hurt," he taunted. He folded his arms and snickered at Charlie.

"Please don't EVER do that again," Katie told Loogar. "That was the most horrible thing I have ever seen. Ugh!" She shuddered. She could not forget the image. She buried her face in her hands and shook her head, trying really hard to forget.

"A genie can grant any wish," Loogar said, "even horrible wishes. I must grant the wish that I hear. I even grant wishes that I do not like. But this wish was quite fun." He smirked.

"It wasn't fun for me. Now my nose really hurts," Charlie said.

"A small price to entertain your prince," Loogar sneered.

"You should be nicer to your friends," Katie scolded.

"Perhaps," Loogie sighed.

"We could have more fun if I felt better," Charlie groaned.

"Your sneezing is quite annoying. A wish might help," Loogie suggested.

"Really? OK, then I wish I wasn't sick," Charlie said.

Instantly his nose cleared. He felt well again. "Wow! That worked!" He breathed deeply through his nose. "Thank you, Loogie!"

"I suppose you are welcome. You must tell Wizard Hendrick that I have done this good deed for you. A peasant hardly deserves such kindness," Loogar scoffed. "Certainly this will speed me to my freedom from your nose."

4.

Cool Wishes

They finished their toast and cocoa. Katie stood up from the table. "Come on, Loogie. Now that Charlie's feeling better, let's go play. What other sorts of magic can you do? Have you granted any cool wishes?"

"ALL of my magic is spectacular," Loogar huffed. "Your peasant friend's wishes are not always so."

"I make good wishes," Charlie retorted. "And we've done lots of cool things. We traveled back through time, remember? Loogie turned me into a dragon, too. Being a dragon was awesome! Maybe you could make me a dragon again."

"Someone would see you, Charlie. It's pretty

hard to hide a dragon," Katie warned.

"True. But I could be smaller this time. Watch this—I wish I was a tiny dragon!"

Suddenly Charlie became a dragon the size of a small bird. His breath was like the flame of a

candle. Loogar had also shrunk in size. He floated in front of Charlie.

Katie laughed. "You're so little!"

"Cool, huh? I wish you could ride on my back," he roared (though it sounded like a tiny chirp).

Instantly Katie appeared as a tiny figure on Charlie's dragon back. Loogar blew backward as Charlie took flight. He grabbed Katie and wrapped his arms around her waist.

"This is very undignified," Loogar grumbled.

"Are you kidding? This is great!" Katie shrieked with delight. "Hang on, Loogie!"

They flew around the living room. It was a cozy place with cushy sofas and a dozen soft pillows. A large stone fireplace filled the corner of the room.

"Your home is rather pleasant, peasant," Loogar said. "Though it is certainly unlike my Garoth Castle."

"Hey, let's go check out your miniature castles, Charlie," Katie suggested. Charlie had built very detailed model castles from pebbles and concrete. "We're so small that they will seem like real castles."

"Great idea!" Charlie pumped his wings and pushed his way upstairs. He swooped down the hall toward his room. Grubbs, his orange tabby cat, leaped for them as they flew overhead. His paw narrowly missed swatting Charlie's tail.

Charlie flew into one of the castle courtyards. He circled around and then swooped upward to perch at the top of the castle's keep. Katie wrapped her arms tightly around Charlie's neck.

"This is so cool!" she yelled gleefully.

"Humph! I suppose this IS rather adventurous," Loogar agreed reluctantly.

"You want adventure? I can give you a ride," Charlie said. He jumped off his perch and flew toward the wall, then banked sharply upward. His

feet and tail dragged along the surface as he climbed. Charlie arched his back until he was flying upside down over his bed. Katie let go and fell to the soft bedding below. Loogar released her and his tether snapped him back to Charlie like a bungee cord. He grabbed Charlie's neck and held tight as Charlie landed on the bed.

"That was awesome!" Katie said.

"It was acceptable," Loogar grumbled.

Katie giggled. She thought Loogar's arrogance was funny.

Grubbs jumped up onto the bed to investigate.

"Grubbs, don't eat us!" Katie screeched. The orange tabby cat hissed and backed away.

"I wish we were all normal size again," Charlie said. Instantly Charlie and Katie were sitting on the bed. Loogar floated beside them. Grubbs screeched and leapt away down the hall, his tail bristling with fear.

Charlie's mother called from downstairs.

"Loogar!" Charlie whispered. "Get back in my nose!"

Mrs. Simms climbed the stairs to Charlie's room. "Charlie, you need your rest. Katie will have to go home now."

"I feel OK," Charlie said. But his mother did not know that magic had cured his cold. He knew she would make him rest. He shrugged apologetically at Katie.

"It's OK," she said. "I'll call you tomorrow."

5.

A Very Nasty Cold

Charlie woke up Sunday to bright sunshine. His cold was gone. He felt great! And Loogar wasn't tickling his nose as he usually did.

"Are you awake?" Charlie asked aloud. He rubbed his nose three times to call on Loogie.

The prince burst forth, but instead of curling upward on a wisp of smoke, he sank down and flopped backward. Loogar hung there, dangling from Charlie's nose.

"Loogie, you're still sleeping," Charlie laughed. "Wake up!" Charlie shook him, but Loogar just flopped and moaned. Charlie grabbed Loogar's hand and pulled him up.

Loogar was awake, sort of. But his eyes were

puffy and his nose was red and drippy. Loogie the booger genie had slimy boogers of his own.

"What happened to you?" Charlie asked. He handed him a tissue.

Loogar did not look like a genie at all. He certainly did not look like a prince. He looked like a very sick little boy.

The prince groaned as he wiped his nose. "Hendrick must have cast a spell to kill me. He is a horrible wizard. I feel as though I will die soon. Farewell. You have been a good friend, for a peasant."

Charlie laughed. "You're not dying, Loogie. You have my cold."

Loogar shook his head. "I am not cold. I feel very hot." He sniffled and coughed as he spoke.

Charlie laughed again. "Yes, that's a fever. When you have a cold, you get a fever."

"Do not mock me, peasant. Surely this is a wizard's spell. I will die soon."

"No, you won't die. Try blowing your nose. That makes me feel better when I have a cold."

Loogar blew his nose as Charlie had suggested. But he did not hold the tissue tightly. His boogers blew out of the tissue and hit Charlie's cheek.

Charlie winced. "Yuck! That's not funny." He grabbed another tissue and wiped the boogers off.

Loogar began to laugh but sneezed instead. Of course he sneezed all over Charlie. He sneezed over and over.

Charlie held up his hands to block the

sneezes. Too late—he was already covered with spittle. "Gross! You sneezed all over me!"

"This is not my fault. I told you, the wizard has cast a spell upon me," Loogar said through another sneeze.

Charlie shoved tissues into his hand. "Stop sneezing on me. Use these to cover your mouth when you sneeze. Cold medicine might help if you could take it. But it would just pass through you to the floor since you have no belly."

"Medicine would not help me. Can you not see that I am dying? Yet you must remind me that I have not eaten in 805 years?"

"Sorry, Loogie. I wish the wizard were here. Maybe he could make you feel better," Charlie said.

Suddenly snow blew in through the open window. "Snow? Blizzard!" Charlie realized the genie had not heard him clearly. "No, Loogie. I wish the WIZARD were here, not BLIZZARD! It's not winter. It's not supposed to snow."

The snow stopped and Charlie heard a

wonderful sound. He ran to his window and looked out. An ice cream truck was rolling slowly down the street. Its tinny music warbled and crackled.

"Quick! Get back in your bottle, Loogie!" The prince disappeared into Charlie's nose. Charlie grabbed his piggy bank and shook out a dollar. He ran downstairs and out to the curb.

6.

The Ice Cream Truck

The ice cream truck stopped in front of Charlie. Several neighborhood children ran toward it. Katie was with them.

"Hey, Charlie! Feeling better?" she asked.

"Yes, but now Loogie is sick," Charlie replied.

"Poor Loogie. Hey, look! Tom is here."

Tom lived a few streets away. The three of them were best friends. They spent lots of time together.

"I got here at the right time," Tom said. "I love ice cream!"

They waited for the truck's window to open. The other children pressed in behind them. Finally the window opened, and Charlie found himself face-to-face with the old wizard.

The wizard scowled at Charlie. "I might have known," he said.

Charlie jumped back. "Hendrick!" He choked out the name.

"Charlie, what's wrong?" Katie asked. "Who's Hendrick?"

Charlie whispered in her ear so the other children could not hear.

"Loogie's wizard?" Katie whispered back.

Charlie nodded. He grabbed her arm and pulled her aside.

"What's going on?" Tom asked. "Don't you guys want ice cream?" He licked his lips as the wizard handed him a chocolate ice cream cone.

"We're OK," they replied together. "We'll get ice cream in a minute."

"You can wait if you want. I'm eating mine before it melts," Tom said. He nibbled eagerly at the ice cream.

The other children bought their ice cream and left. Finally the three friends were alone with the wizard.

"Why are you here?" Charlie asked Hendrick.

"Well, I did not leave England of my own desire," he replied. "I was preparing my dinner—England is several hours ahead, you know. Perhaps you made another of your foolish wishes?"

"I did wish to see you. I guess that's why you're here," Charlie said.

"Yes. That is why I was suddenly driving this horrible truck. Children were running after me. Being mobbed by hungry children is very upsetting," the wizard grumbled. "Why am I here?"

"Loogar has a cold. He needs your help," Charlie pleaded.

Hendrick smiled wickedly. "The little snot is

suffering, then?"

Charlie nodded.

"What are you guys talking about?" Tom asked.

Charlie quickly looked around him. The other children had returned to their homes.

"Promise you won't tell anyone?" Charlie asked Tom.

"Yeah, sure. Friends keep secrets," Tom replied.

"You can't tell ANYONE," Charlie insisted. Then he rubbed his nose and Loogar trickled out in a river of smoke.

Tom grimaced as he watched the smoke waft out of Charlie's nose. "Gross! What is THAT?"

Finally Loogar appeared. He flopped onto the ice cream counter and moaned.

Tom jumped. "What—WHO is that?" He poked at Loogar. The prince did not move, just moaned louder.

The wizard started to snicker. Soon he threw his head back and laughed out loud.

"Evil wizard," Loogar groaned. "Why have you cast this spell to kill me?"

"Can't you help him?" Charlie asked.

The wizard sighed. "I suppose I might brew a wellness potion," Hendrick said. "Of course, I have no laboratory. Magical ingredients are impossible to find these days. And I have not brewed a potion in three hundred years. This could prove very interesting."

"Loogie can get you the ingredients," Charlie said. "I just have to wish, right?"

"Yes, I suppose that could work. Your genie friend certainly knows about magical ingredients," Hendrick said dryly. Loogar had tainted many of Hendrick's potions. The prince was quite familiar with the ingredients for brewing them. "Make your wish."

"I wish the ice cream truck was a wizard's laboratory," Charlie said boldly.

In a flash, tubs of ice cream were replaced by a toilet and sink.

Hendrick and Charlie were dumbstruck. Tom and Katie laughed. Hendrick laughed too. "Convenient, I should think," he said.

Charlie realized what had gone wrong. "That's not a LABoratory. Loogie, you made a LAVatory!" he said. "You can't hear very well with your cold. I wished for a wizard's laboratory!" Suddenly a giant lizard appeared in Charlie's arms. The lizard's head was bandaged. It drooled all over Charlie.

Katie's hands flew to her cheeks. "No! Loogie, Charlie didn't want a lizard with a lobotomy, he wanted a wizard's laboratory!"

The lizard disappeared. The toilet and sink

disappeared. Then cauldrons appeared, filled with steaming brew.

Hendrick nodded his approval. "Now this is all very lovely," he said. "But I cannot brew potions without magical ingredients. Magical ingredients come from magical creatures, and magical creatures are all extinct in your time. That is why magic has disappeared. That is why people now use science. It would be impossible to stock a wizard's laboratory here."

"Not impossible. I just have to wish," Charlie said. He grinned broadly at Hendrick. "I wish we had every magical ingredient imaginable."

Magical creatures of every size and sort—griffins, fauns, fairies, and so many others—swarmed the ice cream truck. A pure white unicorn shook its horn at Katie. A dragon nuzzled at Tom's chest, then blasted fire into the air. A centaur pushed his way to the window and demanded a chocolate ice cream cone.

"I would not think a centaur would eat ice cream," Hendrick said.

"Give me the cone and don't tell my wife," the centaur replied.

"Loogar, I wanted magical ingredients, not magical creatures!" Charlie protested.

Bowls appeared along the shelves, filled with all sorts of magical ingredients. Shaved unicorn horn, lizard eyes, and dried salamander tails were just a few. Loogie had filled the wizard's laboratory, but the creatures still remained. They milled around lazily, licking ice cream from their lips.

7.

Forgotten Magic

The old ice cream truck began to shudder noisily. The truck had idled all the while Hendrick handed out ice cream. Now it had run out of gas. It continued to shudder noisily for several moments, then backfired with a loud pop like a gunshot when the engine died.

The creatures jumped at the sound and went stampeding through the neighborhood. A flock of flying pigs squealed and flew away north. Several griffins flew south.

"No!" Charlie screamed, but his voice was drowned out by the roar of the stampede. "Loogie, you have to get rid of these creatures. People will see them. People will freak out!"

Loogar just moaned.

"I think we have exhausted his magic," said Hendrick. "I am too old and slow to stop so many creatures. Only your genie can fix this mess. But first we will have to fix HIM."

The wizard threw a pinch of powdered unicorn horn into a steaming cauldron. He added some very gooey dragon drool and stirred in a bit of crushed rose petal. When a large bubble grew on the potion, he tapped it with his wand. The bubble exploded into crystals. Hendrick poured the crystals into a tiny glass and added fairy tears. He swirled the mixture, then handed the glass to Loogar.

"Won't the potion just pass through Loogie?" Charlie asked.

Hendrick snickered. "Yes, it will. Genies do not eat, but the magic of the potion should still work." He nudged Loogar. "Drink this and you will feel much better."

Loogar smelled it and made a face. "You could at least make it smell good, wizard."

"Things that are good for you do not always smell or taste good, my princely snot. Hold your nose while you drink," said the wizard.

Loogar held his nose and drank. The potion passed through him just as Hendrick said it would. But soon his nose cleared. His fever cooled. He felt better.

The prince floated upward. He folded his arms across his chest and glared at Tom. "Who are you, peasant?"

"Um...I'm Tom. What are you?"

"Tom, this is Loogie. He's a genie," Katie answered for him.

"I am a prince," Loogar corrected her.

"Seriously? A genie? Awesome!" Tom said. "But why is he stuck in your nose?"

"He's stuck in my nose by magic," Charlie said.

"Wicked magic," Loogar groaned and glared at Hendrick.

"Weird!" Tom said. He pointed at the wizard. "So who's the old guy?"

"That's Hendrick," Charlie replied. "He's the wizard who turned Loogie into a genie eight hundred and five years ago."

"You're eight hundred years old?" Tom asked the wizard.

"Nine hundred and eighteen, actually," replied Hendrick.

"Wow! Do all wizards live as long as you?" Tom asked.

"No," replied Hendrick. "I should have died hundreds of years ago. Wizards only live four or five hundred years. I believe I am here because of Loogar. I swore to his father that I would look after the prince. A wizard's promise has magic and I must honor my promise. I suppose that magic has kept me alive. I have not seen another wizard in almost five hundred years. I believe I am the only one left."

Suddenly Loogar flopped back onto the ice cream counter.

"Loogie! What happened?" Katie asked. Loogar replied with a loud snore.

"Perhaps I have forgotten the potion," Hendrick said. "As I said, I have not brewed a potion in three hundred years. Much can be forgotten in that time."

"Maybe your potions don't work the same on genies," Charlie suggested.

"This could be true," Hendrick said. "I have never given a wellness potion to a genie. Why would I? I have only known one other genie. The king's genie, Tildor, was evil. He was imprisoned for evil wizardry. He did not deserve the mercy of a wellness potion."

"Can't you do something for Loogie?" Charlie asked.

Hendrick shrugged. "I can offer no more help. Loogar must fight his illness the old-fashioned way—with rest and sleep." He waved his wand and disappeared with the ice cream truck.

8.

Glass-Eyed Peasant

Drool seeped from the corner of Loogar's mouth as he snored loudly. He hung upside down from Charlie's nose, sleeping. Charlie just stood there while Tom and Katie stared at the genie. The three of them felt helpless.

"Maybe no one will see the creatures," Charlie suggested hopefully. Most of the creatures had fled. Charlie looked around and saw only a faun, the unicorn, and a few fairies.

"They're sort of hard to miss," Katie said. "Can't

Loogie do something?"

"Of course not. Look at him." Charlie shook his head. Loogar flopped back and forth. "He's caused enough trouble already. He needs rest. Get back in your bottle, Loogar. Rest until you feel better."

The bottle slowly pulled Loogar into Charlie's nose. The prince continued to sleep.

Katie looked up at the sky. Two griffins circled like birds of prey.

"Those griffins look pretty hungry," Katie said. "We shouldn't hang around here. We'd better go inside."

"You're right," Charlie said. "Let's go." Charlie hurried toward his house. Tom and Katie followed.

Tom glanced up. The griffins had seen the movement and dove after them. Tom saw the beasts speeding toward them. "Yikes! Hurry!" he yelled. They ran into Charlie's house as the griffins swooped low over their heads, then soared skyward.

Charlie led them upstairs to his room.

"That was really close!" Katie breathed.

Tom tripped on his shoelaces and fell into Charlie's room. He almost knocked over the model castles as he tumbled to the floor. His glasses fell off and he fumbled around for them. When he put them back on, Tom spotted an ancient medicine

bottle under the bed. "Hey, Charlie, where did you get this? It looks really old." Tom picked up the bottle.

Charlie shrugged.

"Maybe if I clean it a bit," Tom said. It was a very dirty bottle. He rubbed the bottle against his sleeve. A wisp of green smoke floated slowly out of the neck. The wisp grew to a large green cloud. Suddenly the cloud exploded. Tom nearly dropped the bottle.

A plump green genie floated in front of them. He did not look friendly.

"Wow! Cool!" Tom shouted. "Another genie!"

The genie pounded his fists against the sides of his round belly. He clenched his teeth and furrowed his brow. He looked quite angry.

Charlie felt a chill creep up his spine. He remembered Loogar's stories of Tildor, the evil wizard. Tildor had destroyed villages. He had hurt thousands of people before Hendrick locked him in a bottle. Tildor had become a genie just as Loogar had. That was his punishment. Now it seemed he was here. This had to be Tildor.

"Tom, I don't think this genie is a good genie," Charlie warned.

Tildor bellowed, "Why have I been locked in my bottle? Where is King Ardin?" He saw Tom holding his bottle. "Ahhh! A new master, perhaps." The genie grinned wickedly. "That would mean that

Ardin, my old master, has perished. I hope his death was a slow and painful one."

He swooped in threateningly and came nose-to-nose with Tom. "You will be a better master. You will set me free, young glass-eyed peasant."

Charlie swallowed hard. He felt he couldn't breathe. "You must be Tildor," he croaked.

Tildor spun to face Charlie. "The young peasant has heard of the great Tildor. What do you know of me, peasant?" He lunged toward Charlie and waited for him to answer.

Charlie replied shakily, "Hendrick has said you are a wicked genie."

"Not wicked," Tildor said. "I merely seek justice for my enslavement. Where is that wizard? I will seek my justice with him."

"I've seen the wizard," Tom said cheerfully. "I can help you find him."

Tildor spun around on Tom. He faked a smile. "Can you now, glass-eyed master?"

"No, he can't!" Charlie said. "Send him back into his bottle, Tom."

"But he's my genie," Tom said. "I am his master." He held the bottle close to his chest.

"Tildor is no one's genie. He's evil," Charlie said. "He'll hurt all of us or worse if he has a chance."

"But he says that I'm his master. That means he has to grant my wishes," Tom said.

Charlie looked terrified. Tom could see he was scared. At last he relented. "Tildor, could you please go back into your bottle for now?" he asked timidly.

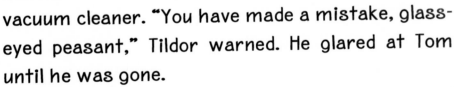

Slowly the bottle began to pull Tildor back inside. It seemed like a powerful vacuum cleaner. "You have made a mistake, glass-eyed peasant," Tildor warned. He glared at Tom until he was gone.

Charlie took the bottle from Tom. "How did Tildor's bottle get here?" he asked.

"Maybe Loogar brought him here with the

magical creatures," Katie suggested.

"Maybe. But wouldn't his bottle have been near the ice cream truck?" Charlie asked. Katie shrugged. They didn't know that Loogie's nanny, Miss Bellediddy, had slipped the bottle into Charlie's pocket on his last adventure. They had gone back in time to save her, and she had sent Tildor home with them.

Charlie's mother called from downstairs, "Charlie! I need you to come do your chores. Your friends will have to go home now."

Charlie looked helplessly at Tom and Katie.

"We'll see you tomorrow," Katie said.

"Can I have Tildor's bottle?" Tom asked.

Charlie shook his head. "He's too dangerous. He stays with me."

"Fine," Tom sighed. He really wanted his own genie to grant his wishes.

9.

When Pigs Fly

The next morning, Charlie watched a pair of hawks circle high above his house. At least he hoped they were hawks. He rode to school with his father, who was also the school principal. It was a pleasant morning. He did not know the frightful day it would become.

Tom and Katie waited for him in the classroom. Their classmates had not yet arrived.

"Have you seen any of the magical creatures today?" Charlie asked.

"I thought I saw the unicorn," Katie replied. "But it was just a flash of white. I couldn't be sure."

"Griffins flew over my house," Tom said.

"Good thing my mom didn't see them. She would freak out!"

"Is Loogie well enough to do something about them?" Katie asked.

"I haven't tried to wake him. I think he's still asleep. When he wakes up, he always tickles my nose," Charlie explained. "He hasn't done that yet today."

"Wake him up," Katie said. "We need him. We have to send the creatures away before they hurt someone."

"OK, I'll try," Charlie said hesitantly. He rubbed his nose and waited. Several moments passed. Finally Loogar dribbled out like a wet booger and hung upside down from Charlie's nose. He was still sleeping.

Tom grimaced. "Ew! Gross!" He backed away from the genie.

"Loogie is still sick," Charlie said. "We can't ask him for anything now. He might mix up more wishes. His magic could make things worse. He needs to get well."

The sleeping genie jiggled back and forth as Charlie spoke. Then he awoke. He was not very agreeable.

"What do you want, Charlie?" the prince moaned. He lifted his head to look at Charlie. His eyes were puffy and red. His cheeks were pale.

"Hey, you called me 'Charlie'! You didn't call me 'peasant'!"

"What does it matter what I called you, peasant? I am dying!"

"Oh, Loogie, you're really sick, aren't you," Katie cooed.

"No, I am dying," he groaned. "Why did you call on me, peasant?" He sniffled and coughed, then let his head down.

"To see how you are feeling," Charlie replied.

"I am dying. Can you not see? Let me die in peace," Loogar grumbled, and slowly disappeared into his bottle.

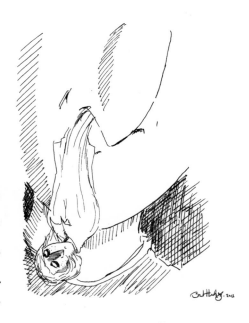

"I hope he gets well soon," Katie said. "We need him. The griffins are getting hungry. Hendrick said that only Loogie can make the creatures disappear."

Other children entered the classroom. The three friends scattered to their desks.

Their teacher, Miss Turner, arrived. She smiled warmly at her students. "Good morning, children!"

Outside the window, Katie saw movement. A tiny creature buzzed and tapped the glass. It looked like a hummingbird, but when Katie squinted to see more clearly, she realized it was a fairy. The tiny creature turned and sped away when it saw her. Katie bit her lip and turned back to Miss Turner.

"Today we're going to learn about physics," Miss Turner told them. "Hundreds of years ago, people believed in magic and witchcraft."

Charlie, Tom, and Katie looked at each other with wide eyes. They silently hoped that Miss Turner had not seen the magical creatures.

"They thought that for people to fly, they must use magic," Miss Turner continued. "A man named Bernoulli proved differently." She drew an airplane on the board. "Bernoulli showed us how to create lift. Lift is what makes planes fly."

"What makes pigs fly?" asked little Jenny Lynn.

"Jenny Lynn, are you being fresh?" Miss Turner asked.

Jenny Lynn shook

her head. She pointed toward the window. Miss Turner looked. The other children looked too, but there was nothing to see.

"I saw a pig flying outside the window," Jenny Lynn said.

Charlie had seen the pig too, pressing its little pink snout against the glass. He breathed a sigh of relief when it flew away. No one would believe Jenny Lynn. She was Miss Turner's favorite, and for that, the other students disliked her. His classmates laughed.

Miss Turner looked concerned. "Jenny Lynn, go see the nurse. Tell her what you saw."

"But he was really there!" Jenny Lynn insisted.

"I'm sure that you saw him," Miss Turner said. She placed her hand on Jenny Lynn's forehead. "Not too warm. But you should go see the nurse."

The other children snickered. Jenny Lynn left with tears in her eyes.

"Class, it's not nice to laugh at Jenny Lynn,"

Miss Turner scolded. "She may be very sick. Now, it's time for recess. Let's all go outside. It's a beautiful day. We should take some time to enjoy the sunshine."

Charlie, Tom, and Katie shared frightened looks. Outside was the last place they wanted to be today. That was where the creatures were, and some of them were monsters.

10.

Creatures Large and Small

The sun was bright and warm as the children hurried out into the schoolyard. Charlie, Tom, and Katie looked for magical creatures, but they saw none. High overhead, a hawk circled lazily.

"I brought my hacky sack," Tom said. "Want to kick it around some?"

Katie shrugged. "Sure."

Tom pulled out the brightly colored sack of beans. He bounced it off his knee to his toe and kicked it to her. Katie kicked it sideways up to her elbow, then her head. She butted it over to

Charlie. It landed at his feet. Charlie wasn't paying attention to the game. He was staring up at the hawk.

"Charlie, are you going to play with us?" Katie asked. "You'll have to stop staring at the birds."

"It looks like a hawk," Charlie said. "But I don't think it is." He pointed toward the sky.

Tom and Katie looked up. The animal was closer now. It was plain to see that it was not a hawk. Its head was far too large and its tail much too long. And its tail did not fan like a bird's tail. It was long and snakelike.

Suddenly the creature dove toward the schoolyard. "It's a griffin!" Charlie said. "He's moving in fast!"

He ran toward the shrubs by the school building. He hid behind them and quickly rubbed his nose. The prince appeared.

"What do you want, peasant?" he groaned.

"Loogar, you have to help. A griffin is about to attack the school," Charlie said. He looked out at the schoolyard. A boy was playing alone. Charlie saw the griffin plummet toward him.

"He's after that boy. I wish he would stop!" Charlie said frantically.

The boy stopped moving. He didn't look up. He didn't see the griffin. He just froze where he was.

Loogar hadn't made the griffin stop— he'd made the boy stop.

The griffin approached. Still the boy didn't move. The griffin watched carefully. Tasty griffin treats moved. This boy did not move like a griffin treat. At the last moment the beast flapped his wings and soared skyward, leaving the motionless boy below.

Charlie sighed with relief.

"I don't think the griffin is the only creature here," Katie said. "Look at the woods."

She pointed to the thick woods behind the school. Large eyes and small ones glowed among the trees. There were hundreds of them! They stared and blinked like Christmas lights. Loogar's magical creatures had come to school.

"Why are they here?" Charlie asked. "Loogie, why are the magical creatures here?"

"Magical. features? What features?" Loogar asked.

"Not features, Loogie. Creatures!" Charlie said. "Loogie, you have to get well! We need your help!"

The creatures began to emerge from the woods. They hopped, waddled, walked, and slithered into the schoolyard. Creatures large and small were everywhere!

"What have you sent to kill me now, wizard?" Loogar whined. His eyes widened, and then he disappeared into his bottle.

The children froze with fear as the creatures crowded in. The two-headed lion at the front of the pack was particularly fearsome. He roared

and shook his heads. His tail snapped back and forth like a whip.

A small child screamed and ran. Then all of the children were screaming frantically. They ran from the creatures and swarmed into the school like bees. Katie, Tom, and Charlie followed. A flock of fairies zipped through the doorway over their heads. Charlie slammed the door behind them.

11.
Hide and Seek

Charlie, Tom, and Katie leaned against the door, panting heavily. They watched the other children run down the halls and into the classrooms.

The fairies buzzed over them. One flew at Charlie and kicked him in the head. Another slapped his face. "Hey! What's that for?" Charlie winced as a fairy stabbed his ear with a tiny spear.

"Your magic drew us from our homes," a fairy squeaked. "Send us back!"

"I can't send you back. My genie is sick. I have to wait until he is well," Charlie explained.

"We don't care about your genie slave. You brought us here. Send us home!" they screeched.

Outside, the magical creatures crowded around the school building. The griffins pecked at the doors; the flying pigs rutted around the bushes. Then a minotaur pushed his way through the crowd. Standing upright, his huge bull's head towered over the other creatures. He threw his shoulder against the door. The jamb splintered and snapped and the doors flew open. The creatures stampeded inside.

Charlie, Tom, and Katie ducked into the girls'

bathroom. The fairies slipped in over their heads.

"Ew! Why are we in the girls' bathroom?" Tom complained.

"It was the nearest door," Charlie argued.

In the hallway the minotaur led the raid. Like a general, he sent the creatures to search the school for the magic that had summoned them. They wanted to go home, and only magic could send them there. The fauns searched the classrooms while the centaur searched the offices. The dragon headed for the bathrooms.

"Shhhhh!" Katie hushed them. They heard scratching at the bathroom door. It was the dragon.

"Let's hide in the stalls," Charlie whispered. They rushed to the toilet stalls. Each of them climbed onto a toilet and crouched to hide. It was a frightening game of hide-and-seek.

Claws fumbled with the door handle. The door opened and the dragon stuck his head inside. The door closed on his neck. The dragon screeched and blasted fire into the bathroom. He struggled to pull his head out of the doorway. Finally he slipped his head out and the door slammed shut. He thumped the walls with his tail and turned to the boys' bathroom. The three friends listened as he opened that door. It closed on him too. The dragon roared and smashed his tail into the girls' bathroom door. Charlie heard it splinter. He thought it would break. But at last the dragon lumbered away and it was quiet. Each of the three children breathed a sigh of relief.

12.

A Genie to Save Us

The fairies renewed their attack on Charlie and he swatted them away. The three friends huddled together, terrified that the creatures would find them. "Send us home!" the fairies squeaked. Katie pressed Charlie to ask for Loogie's help.

"Loogie is too sick to help," Charlie said. "He'll just make things worse." He paused. "I do have an idea, but you're not going to like it. We have to get to my locker. Tildor's bottle is there."

"You brought Tildor to school?" Katie asked.

"I was afraid to leave him at home. Mom might find him," Charlie explained. He opened the door and poked his head into the hallway. Tom pulled him back inside.

"I should go get Tildor," Tom said. "They're looking for you. Also, Tildor's magic only works for me, right?"

Tom was right. Tildor was his genie—Tom was his master. He had awakened Tildor from his bottle. Now Tildor could grant only Tom's wishes.

"Are you sure you want to go? The creatures might eat you alive," Charlie warned.

"I'll be careful," Tom said. "What's your locker combo?"

Charlie gave it to him: 18-23-40. Tom repeated the numbers under his breath and slipped out of the bathroom.

The animals had all but left the main corridor. Only a few jackalopes, rabbits with antlers, hopped around the floor. Tom sprinted for Charlie's locker. He whispered the combination to himself as he ran. The jackalopes bellowed an alarm that rattled Tom's eardrums and raised the hair on his neck.

Tom skidded to a stop at Charlie's locker. Quickly he spun the lock to the right numbers. The lock popped open. He snatched Charlie's backpack and fled.

The hallway to the bathroom was blocked by creatures that had responded to the jackalopes' alarm. Tom ducked into the janitor's closet and locked the door.

"Tildor, you have to do what I say," he whispered to the bottle. "It doesn't matter if you're evil. You can't disobey me. You have to save us." Tom rubbed the bottle until finally Tildor eased his way out. The genie folded his arms and rested them on his large belly. He glared at Tom.

It was a small closet. There was no room for Tom to back away. Tildor was nose-to-nose with him.

"What do you want, glass-eyed peasant?"

Tildor bellowed. His voice was deep, like low, rolling thunder. He poked at Tom's glasses. Tom froze in terror as the genie loomed near him.

"Out with it, runt!" Tildor barked. He glared until Tom shook in his shoes.

"I-I-I'm y-y-your m-m-master," Tom stuttered. "Y-y-you have to do what I say."

"Then tell me what you wish, glass-eyed MASTER," Tildor growled.

"I-I-I w-w-wish the creatures would leave the school," Tom whimpered.

"As you wish, MASTER," he grumbled.

Out in the hall, mice scurried from the heating vents and joined the stampede. Tom's wish had not specified which creatures should leave. Tom could hear the larger creatures banging into walls. The sounds faded as they stampeded down the hall and outside.

Tom breathed a sigh of relief. Out in the hall there was silence. Then cheers from the children pierced the air.

"Th-th-thank you, Tildor," Tom said.

"Humph! If there is nothing else—?" Before Tildor finished, he whooshed back into his bottle.

13.

Twisting Wishes

"I think the creatures are gone," Katie whispered.

"Tom must have made a wish," Charlie agreed. "Maybe Tildor isn't as bad as Hendrick claims."

Katie gingerly pushed the bathroom door open. The creatures were indeed gone. Children had gathered in the hallway. They looked both scared and amazed.

"Do you think they came from the zoo?" Charlie heard one girl ask.

"They came out of the woods. They were wild animals," responded a goofy, red-haired boy.

"Nuh-uh. Did you see the two-headed lion? It

must have been a circus."

Katie walked past the gossiping children. She went to the school entrance and opened the door.

A wall of creatures pressed against the open doorway. The two-headed lion snarled at her. Katie screamed. The creatures screeched and screamed and roared in response. But they did not move.

"They're not gone, Charlie! What do we do?" she asked. "We can't go outside."

"Send us home!" the fairies squeaked. "We want to go home!"

All of the creatures nodded. "We want to go home!" they echoed.

"Loogie will have to send you home. He just can't yet. He's too sick to do magic," Charlie said.

"Please leave the school. Be patient. Loogie will send you home when he is well." Charlie closed the door.

"We want to go now!" the centaur bellowed, shaking the door.

"What are we going to do? We can't leave them out there," Katie said.

"I don't know," Charlie replied helplessly. "I wish Hendrick were here."

There was a knock at the door. Katie opened it, and there stood Hendrick on the stoop. The

creatures crowded against him. The two-headed lion slobbered on his head.

"Charlie! I think Loogar heard you. Hendrick is here," Katie said.

Tom hurried over to join them,

carrying Tildor's bottle. Hendrick saw it and furrowed his brow. "Be careful with that bottle, young friend. It is quite dangerous. Do you know what is in there?"

"Yes, it's Tildor. He sent the animals out of the school. He's not evil like you said. He just misunderstood my wish."

"Oh, he understood you. He twisted your wish," Hendrick explained. "He answered your wish literally. Your genie tricked you. You are lucky he wasn't able to use your wish to destroy you and your friends."

"But I wished for the animals to leave the school," Tom said.

"And as you can see, they have done that," Hendrick said. "They have left the school building."

"But the creatures want to go home," Charlie said. "Home is several hundred years ago."

"Yes, it is," Hendrick agreed.

"So let's send them home," Charlie said. He led them outside among the creatures. The creatures did not move.

"Release your genie," Hendrick said to Tom.

Tom rubbed Tildor's bottle. The genie appeared in a puff of green smoke. He saw Hendrick and swooped in at him.

"What is it YOU want, wizard? I belong to the boy now. Your king does not control me any longer," Tildor fumed at Hendrick, seething with hatred.

"You will not control this boy, Tildor. He is smarter than that. Now grant his wish and do not twist his words," Hendrick warned. He turned to Tom. "Your words must be very clear," he said seriously. "There can be no room for misinterpretation. If there is, Tildor will use your wish to his advantage. Do you understand?"

Tom nodded solemnly.

"Good. The creatures would like to go home. Wish for them to go home," Hendrick instructed.

"OK. I wish—"

"Wait!" Hendrick cautioned. "How will you state your wish?"

"I will wish for them to go home," Tom replied.

"But to which home? He could send them to your home if you are not careful. You must wish them to their home."

"OK. I wish the creatures would go back to their home," Tom said.

The creatures disappeared at once. There was no sign that they had ever been there.

Suddenly the mice that had run out of the school now came scurrying toward them. They slipped around the children and wriggled themselves under the door. They too were headed home. They lived in the school.

Inside, they heard Miss Turner scream. Charlie threw open the door. The mice brushed by Miss Turner's ankles. They disappeared into the grates and closets and cracks in the walls.

"Charlie! You're all right!" his father said. He grabbed Charlie and hugged him tightly.

"Hi, Dad," Charlie said. "We're fine." He wriggled out of his father's arms.

Mr. Simms let go reluctantly. "I thought maybe those animals had hurt you, or worse. I'm so glad you're all right. Who is your friend?" He motioned toward the wizard.

"Hendrick," the wizard introduced himself. He held out a withered hand to Charlie's father. "I'm a groundskeeper here."

"I don't recognize you as one of our groundskeepers," Mr. Simms said.

"I only started today," Hendrick replied.

"It's not always this crazy here. Do you know where all of the zoo animals and people in costume came from? And where did they disappear to?" Charlie's father asked.

Charlie shrugged.

Hendrick brightened. "Zoo animals? Yes, I suppose they could have been. Perhaps more likely it was a circus. That might explain the people in costume."

"That could be," Mr. Simms agreed. He was thoughtful a moment, then added, "Do I really want to know?"

"Perhaps not," Hendrick replied. "But they did leave a mess behind. I shall clean up."

14.

Speak Clearly

A week passed before Loogar was well again. He had rested in his bottle the whole time, and Charlie missed his friend. It was Saturday morning when he finally tickled Charlie's nose. Charlie scratched and Loogar whooshed out. He wore a very big grin.

"Is it Saturday?" Loogar asked.

"Yes, it's Saturday. Katie is waiting for us out in the yard. Go back in your bottle for now," Charlie said. Loogar disappeared.

"Hi, Charlie!" Katie greeted him as he stepped out of the house. "How's Loogie feeling?"

"He's well again," Charlie said. He looked around and saw no one. He rubbed his nose and Loogar appeared.

"Good morning, maiden." The prince greeted Katie with a smug smile.

"Good morning, Prince Loogar," Katie replied. "Glad to see you are feeling better. No more mixing up Charlie's wishes?"

"The silly peasant has not made any," Loogar huffed. "Perhaps he worries that I will twist wishes as Tildor does."

"You did enough of that while you were sick," Charlie laughed.

"Nonsense! I granted your wishes. You simply did not speak them clearly," Loogar said. He folded his arms across his chest and stuck his nose in the air. Then he winked at Katie.

Katie smiled. "Hendrick DID say that you have to be very clear with your wishes," she reminded Charlie.

Charlie brightened. "Oh my gosh! He did!"

"What is it, Charlie?" Katie asked.

"Loogie, I wished for you to be free. But the wizard's spell prevents your freedom until you do good deeds," Charlie said.

"Well, of course it does," Loogar said. "We have talked about this. Why are you happy about my enslavement? I thought you were my friend."

Charlie smiled. "Loogie, I wish you were not stuck in my nose."

Instantly Loogar's bottle popped out of Charlie's nose.

Katie's hands flew to her face. Loogar did not notice. "We have tried this. I told you, we will have to cut off your nose," the prince huffed.

"Loogie, it WORKED!" Katie said happily.

Loogar looked at Charlie. He realized then that he was no longer tethered to Charlie's nose.

"This is hardly freedom from Hendrick's dreadful spell, Charlie. But I SUPPOSE that you may keep your nose," he said matter-of-factly.

"Hey, you called me 'Charlie' again!"

"Well, of course I did, peasant. You are my friend," Loogar huffed.

Charlie grinned and together they headed for the swings.

CPSIA information can be obtained at www.ICGtesting.com
Printed in the USA
LVOW05s1622230913

353728LV00002B/519/P